You'll lose that bear is ideal for you to use together when your child:

- enjoys looking at b̶ooks a̶nd̶ ̶will join in to sing r̶h̶

- shows inte̶ ̶̶̶̶̶ .̶.ions.

Using *You'll lose ̶*

- Read *You'll lose that bear* to your child. Take time to enjoy the pictures and especially the large foldout illustration in the middle.

- Point to the words as you read, ask what Pip is doing, and tell your child what the words say.

- The story is presented again at the end of the book. Read it aloud and explain that these words are telling you the whole story.

- Look at all the pictures again. Can your child remember any of the words and say them with you?

A catalogue record for this book is available
from the British Library

Published by Ladybird Books Ltd Loughborough Leicestershire UK
Ladybird Books Ltd is a subsidiary of the Penguin Group of companies.

© LADYBIRD BOOKS LTD MCMXCVI

You'll lose
that bear

written by Geraldine Taylor

illustrated by Ann Johns

"Pip," said Jo.

"You'll lose that bear,

And we'll be looking
everywhere."

"He's not lost,
I've put him…"

"WHERE?"

"There!"

"Pip," said Billy.

"You'll lose that bear,

And we'll be looking
everywhere."

"He's not lost,
I've put him…"

"WHERE?"

"There!"

"Jo," said Pip.

"I've lost my bear.

"I told you, Pip,
you'd lose that bear.

Now we can't find
him anywhere."

"Pip," said Dan.

I've found your bear.

He's fast asleep in the

big armchair."

And everyone said,

"Pip, just leave him there!!!"

You'll lose that bear

"Pip," said Jo. "You'll lose that bear,
And we'll be looking everywhere."

"He's not lost, I've put him…"
"WHERE?"
"There!"

"Pip," said Billy. "You'll lose that bear,
And we'll be looking everywhere."

"He's not lost, I've put him…"
"WHERE?"
"There!"

"Jo," said Pip. "I've lost my bear
And I can't find him
ANYWHERE!"

I told you, Pip, you'd lose that bear.
Now we can't find him anywhere."

Pip," said Dan. "I've found your bear.
He's fast asleep in the big armchair."

And everyone said,
Pip, just leave him there!!!"

Here are some ideas for things you might do together, using *You'll lose that bear* as a basis for other activities.

- **Talk about**

  Have you and your child ever lost and found a beloved toy?

  Where did you search?

  How did you feel when the toy was found?

- **Storytelling**

  Use the large foldout picture in the middle of the book to start your own stories about family things that have been lost and found.

  What's the strangest place your child can think of to find a lost toy?

  For example, a toy rabbit in a hot air balloon, a teddy in a cornflake packet.

  Play this as a family game and you'll have the beginnings of some marvellous stories!

- **Rhyme and memory**

  Rhyming words add extra fun and help
  children to remember the story.
  Try reading the story and leaving out
  the rhyming words at the end of each line,
  pausing to see if your child can tell you
  what they are.

- **Reading practice**

  Can your child 'read' the book to you,
  using the pictures to help him?
  Pretend – or memory – reading is a vital
  step on the way to real reading.

  Other storybooks in this series: